LES MISÉRABLES

VICTOR HUGO

www.realreads.co.uk

Retold by Tony Evans
Illustrated by Catty Flores

Text copyright © Tony Evans 2013
Illustrations copyright © Catty Flores 2013
The right of Tony Evans to be identified as author of
this book has been asserted by him in accordance with the
Copyright, Design and Patents Act 1988

First published in 2013
Reprinted 2015

ISBN 978-1-906230-79-1

Printed in China by Wai Man Book Binding (China) Ltd
Designed by Lucy Guenot
Typeset by Bookcraft Ltd, Stroud, Gloucestershire

CONTENTS

THE CHARACTERS

Jean Valjean

When he was a young man Jean Valjean stole a loaf of bread and spent many years in prison. He is still wanted by the police. Will he ever be able to escape from his past?

Inspector Javert

The inspector is a fierce and clever police officer who is determined to track down Jean Valjean. What will happen when the two men meet?

Cosette

When Cosette is eight years old, she is mistreated and forced to work hard all day. Can she ever find happiness?

Marius

Marius is a handsome and honest young student. When he joins the Paris uprising of 1832, he is badly wounded. Will he ever again see the girl he loves?

Monsieur and Madame Thénardier

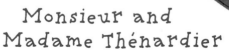

This cruel and selfish couple will do anything for money. Can Jean Valjean rescue Cosette from their clutches?

Éponine

Éponine is frail and lives by begging. She is in love with Marius – but can she save him when he is in danger?

Gavroche

Gavroche is a cheerful and intelligent boy, who manages to survive even though his parents have abandoned him. He lives with other poor children on the streets of Paris. What does his future hold?

LES MISÉRABLES

When *Monsieur le maire* walked through the
streets of the little town of Montreuil-sur-mer,
everyone he met greeted him with a respectful
word or a pleasant smile. Père Madeline – for
that was the name by which he was known –
was a man in his fifties, with a quiet but
determined manner. He was grey-haired with
the tanned face of a farmer or labourer, and
appeared to possess great strength and vigour.
Despite his important position in the town he
dressed simply, in a long tail-coat of plain cloth
and a black broad-brimmed hat.

As the mayor nodded back politely in
answer to the townspeople's greetings, he
thought about how much his life had changed
since his arrival in the town eight years
earlier. He remembered how he had reached
Montreuil-sur-mer late on a December evening
in 1815, tired and hungry, with a pack on his
back and a stout stick in his hand.

During the years that he had lived in the town he had set up a jewellery-making factory, which now employed many of the local workers. He paid them good wages, and had used some of the profits from his business to build two new schools and a hospital. In 1820 he had been appointed as mayor, in recognition of the good works he had done for the town. No one ever asked him about his past, and so only one person in Montreuil-sur-mer knew the truth – the mayor himself. The truth was that his real name was *not* 'Père Madeline'. It was Jean Valjean, and he was wanted by the police.

Jean Valjean's original crime had not been a particularly dreadful one. Indeed, some might say that it had hardly been a crime at all. In 1795, when he was twenty-seven, his sister's children had been starving and there was no work to be had – so in desperation he had stolen a loaf of bread for them. He had been

sentenced to five years hard labour, and after trying to escape he had spent another fourteen years in prison. Following his release in 1815 he had committed another crime. He had stolen a few francs from a young boy – and had regretted it ever since. Although Jean Valjean had long ago decided that he would live an honest life and try to help the poor and the needy, he was still wanted for theft and was on the run from the police. Would they ever track him down?

It was bad luck for the mayor when Inspector Javert moved to the town from Paris. This officer was courageous and single-minded, totally dedicated to fighting crime.

Javert was
suspicious of
Jean Valjean
from the start.
There was
something
about the quiet,
powerful man

which reminded him of a convict he had known
twenty years earlier, and who was still a wanted
man. Inspector Javert decided that he would
go to the Chief of Police in Paris and report his
suspicions. Fortunately for Jean Valjean, the Police
Chief told Javert that it was quite impossible for
the respected mayor of Montreuil-sur-mer to be
the same man that had been on the run eight
years earlier. All Javert could do was to watch
and wait. Jean Valjean knew that Inspector Javert
suspected him, but he hoped that his real identity
would not be discovered.

The mayor of Montreuil-sur-mer always took good care of his employees. One day in January 1823 he discovered that a poor unmarried woman who used to work for him had been forced to send her daughter, Cosette, to be looked after by an innkeeper and his wife, Monsieur and Madame Thénardier. They lived in the village of Montfermeil, not far from Paris. Fantine – the little girl's mother – was very ill, and was not expected to live for much longer. She had heard that Cosette was being mistreated, and Jean Valjean promised to do all he could to help.

Fantine owed a hundred and eighty francs to the innkeeper and his wife. That evening Jean Valjean wrote to Monsieur Thénardier, sending him three hundred francs. He asked the Thénardiers to use the extra money to bring Cosette to Montreuil-sur-mer straight away.

When the letter from Jean Valjean arrived at the inn, Monsieur Thénardier's eyes gleamed at the sight of the money inside. He was a small, thin, sallow-skinned character, with the pointed face and sharp stare of a weasel. He held out the letter to his wife.

'Send the brat home? Oh no we won't! Her mother must have met some rich man – we can make a load of money out of this.'

Madame Thénardier grabbed the letter with her rough, podgy hand. She was tall, red-faced and broad-shouldered, rather like a labourer dressed in a woman's clothes.

'Write back and say the kid's been ill, and we need another five hundred francs for the doctor's bill,' she said with an unpleasant smile. 'Yes – and say she's too sick to travel. We'll hang on to her as long as we can, and then ask for more money for her keep.'

In fact Cosette was not unwell – that is, she had no particular disease or illness. All she was suffering from was neglect. This was hardly surprising, because almost none of the money that her mother had sent the Thénardiers had been spent on food and clothes for Cosette.

After almost two months had passed without Cosette's return, and after several more demands for money had arrived from Monsieur Thénardier, Jean Valjean's patience was exhausted. He promised Fantine that he would travel to the inn to collect Cosette, and make sure that she was properly looked after.

Just as he was about to set off he had a visit from Inspector Javert, who told him that a man from the town of Arras had been identified as Jean Valjean, and arrested.

'You are no longer under suspicion,' he said.

The mayor of Montreuil-sur-mer thought for a moment, then spoke. 'I cannot see an innocent man wrongly convicted. You have arrested the wrong person. *I* am the man you want – I am Jean Valjean.'

Jean Valjean was locked in the town jail in Montreuil-sur-mer, but that night he used his great strength to break one of the bars of the cell window and clamber down from the roof. The next morning he went to the banking-house of Laffitte and withdrew all money he had saved from his business – over 600,000 francs. On his way to the bank, Jean Valjean overheard some very sad news. Cosette's mother, Fantine, had died from her illness the day before.

Very soon afterwards, Jean Valjean was recaptured, but not before he had buried the cash in an iron box in the woods on the edge of the town. He was sentenced to imprisonment for life, and sent to a large jail in the port of Toulon, near the naval dockyard. From that day onwards he would be known as Prisoner number 9430.

It might have been expected that the world would receive no more news of the former mayor of Montreuil-sur-mer. However, almost eight months later the local newspaper in Toulon, in an edition dated the 17th of November 1823, included the following item.

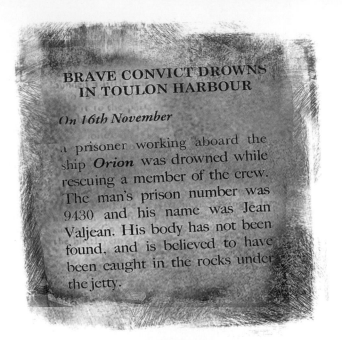

BRAVE CONVICT DROWNS IN TOULON HARBOUR

On 16th November

a prisoner working aboard the ship *Orion* was drowned while rescuing a member of the crew. The man's prison number was 9430 and his name was Jean Valjean. His body has not been found, and is believed to have been caught in the rocks under the jetty.

During the long months of Jean Valjean's imprisonment in Toulon, poor Cosette was still living with Monsieur and Madame Thénardier in the village of Montfermeil. They received no more money for her, but continued to treat her like an unpaid slave.

On Christmas Day in 1823, just after nine o'clock, a knock sounded at the front door of *The Sergeant of Waterloo*, the inn kept by the Thénardiers.

Madame Thénardier glared at Cosette, who was washing the floor. The huge woman's eyes blazed with violent anger.

'Well, answer the door, Miss Useless!' she shouted.

The man who entered the room was well over fifty, with white hair, a lined forehead and a serious expression. However, his powerful figure and lively step suggested that he had the strength of someone much younger. He was dressed in an old but carefully-brushed tall hat, and a clean, threadbare tail-coat.

The visitor looked at the frail little girl who had let him in. Cosette was thin and pale – she was eight years old, but she looked hardly six. Her large eyes, sunken in a sort of shadow, were red with weeping. The corners of her mouth had that curve of sorrow which is seen in desperately unhappy people. The reflections from the fireplace showed up all the angles of her bones, and made her thinness horribly clear. She wore an old cotton dress, and was shivering despite the fire.

The man produced the letter that Fantine had written, but the Thénardiers were much more interested in the large bundle of bank notes – 1500 francs – that he offered them in exchange for Cosette. Monsieur Thénardier was tempted to ask for even more, but there was a determined look in their visitor's eye which made him change his mind.

Madame Thénardier pushed Cosette towards their visitor.

'Go on then, take her. And good riddance!' she said with a cruel smile.

Cosette's saviour left without a word, pausing only to place his coat over the trembling girl's shoulders.

And who was it that had rescued her? It was of course Jean Valjean, who had indeed saved a sailor from drowning, but had managed to swim to safety. His imprisonment in Toulon and his daring and dangerous escape had turned his hair completely white.

It was generally believed that Jean Valjean was dead, but he was determined to keep out of sight until it seemed safe for Cosette and him to live openly again. Although he was able to take as much money as he needed from the box that he had secretly buried in the wood near Montfermeil, Jean Valjean chose to rent two plain and simple rooms in a decayed building known as *la maison Gorbeau* – the Gorbeau tenement. It stood in a run-down part of Paris, where he and Cosette would not be noticed.

Gradually the little girl became healthier, and began to forget about her ill treatment by the Thénardiers. No longer dressed in rags, she began to emerge from misery into life. Children are quick to accept happiness because that is their natural state of mind. She trusted the kind man who had rescued her from her persecutors and, without understanding what had led to her freedom, Cosette was soon entirely content with her new home.

Jean Valjean was also happier than he had ever been before. The promise that he had made to Fantine – that he would protect and look after her daughter – was fulfilled. For the first time in his life he had someone to love and care for.

Jean Valjean had always intended to move to a better house when he felt it safe to do so, but as it turned out he and Cosette had to escape from the Gorbeau tenement much sooner than he had expected. The nosy landlady who collected the rent had become suspicious of her mysterious tenant, who always seemed to have money for a good fire and to give to the poor, despite his simple life.

One evening on a cold night in the February following Cosette's rescue, coming home from a trip to buy food, Jean Valjean noticed a familiar figure on the corner of the street. It was that of a strongly built man, in a

dark tail-coat and black hat, with a serious face like a bulldog. It was Inspector Javert, and there were two other policemen just behind him. Had he been spotted?

Minutes afterwards Jean Valjean was hurrying away from the Gorbeau tenement, with Cosette running beside him. As they turned a corner, they found themselves in a blind alley – buildings stood all around, and the path went no further. Jean Valjean could hear the policemen's footsteps close behind. He climbed up the brick wall in front of them, and reached down to Cosette. Grasping her hands, he pulled her up beside him, and lowered her down on the other side. For the moment they were safe.

Inspector Javert was sure that the man he had chased was Jean Valjean, who had somehow survived when he fell in the harbour at Toulon. But the inspector made a big mistake – he expected the escaped convict and the little girl he had with him to find another cheap lodging. Instead, Jean Valjean rented a pleasant house in the Rue Plumet, a very respectable part of Paris well away from the Gorbeau tenement. He used the name of Monsieur Fauchelevant, and he and Cosette dressed well, and employed a servant.

The inspector's enquiries were unsuccessful. At last it seemed as if Valjean and Cosette could live normal lives, free from fear of capture.

For the next seven years Jean Valjean and Cosette lived quietly and undisturbed in the Rue Plumet. Cosette went to school at a local convent, where she was taken each day by 'Monsieur Fauchelevant'.

In the summer of 1831, on most fine days
the happy pair would walk together in the
Luxembourg Gardens – a large and peaceful
public park in Paris where old and young would
gather to enjoy pleasant walks, sculptures and
fountains. Jean Valjean and Cosette would
often sit side by side on a bench in one of their
favourite spots, near the Rue l'Ouest.

Of the many walkers who passed that place, one in particular soon began to look forward to seeing them. He was a young man called Marius Pontmercy, just twenty-one years old. Marius had quarrelled with his only relative – his grandfather – and was a student with very little money of his own. Each time he saw Cosette, he became more and more attracted to her.

Cosette was now fifteen. The pathetic little girl who had been rescued from the evil Thénardiers seven years earlier was now a tall and beautiful creature. She had wonderful brown hair, flecked with threads of gold, fine skin, long eyelashes and a bewitching face.

Although Cosette did her best not to stare at the young man who often passed their bench, she could not help noticing and admiring him. Soon she began to look forward to his appearance, and would turn her beautiful head towards him with a faint smile on her lips. Encouraged by this, Marius started to sit on a

bench nearby, and would gaze at Cosette while pretending to read a book. He had – almost without realising it – fallen deeply in love, even though he and Cosette had not even exchanged a word, and did not even know each other's names.

Of course by this time Jean Valjean was well aware of what was going on. He knew nothing about Marius, who, as it happened, was an honest, clever and hardworking young gentleman from a good family, but *any* man who was in love with Cosette would have met with Jean Valjean's disapproval. He decided that they would end their visits to the Luxembourg Gardens. Cosette guessed the reason, but was certain that she and the young man would meet again. Surely he could discover her name, and find her house in the Rue Plumet.

When Marius discovered that the old gentleman and his young companion no longer visited the gardens, he did his utmost to find out who they were – but without success. Many people he spoke to knew the couple by sight, but none could say where they lived. Still, Marius did not give up hope. All his friends were on the lookout for the young woman he had described, and he hoped one day that she would be found.

Seven months passed, and Marius had still failed to find Cosette. One afternoon he was sitting at his desk in the little room that he rented in a cheap area of Paris. There was a timid knock on his door – he could guess who it was. The two rooms next to his were occupied by a very poor couple and their sixteen-year-old daughter, Éponine. She would sometimes ask Marius for a 'loan' to buy food for the family, and although he was always short of money he would usually give her a few francs – which were never repaid.

The young woman who stepped into Marius' room was tall and frail, with long bare legs and bony knees, and her dress was ragged. When she saw Marius she smiled, and for a moment a trace of beauty shone out from her careworn face.

'Hello! Can I come in?' She entered the room before he could reply. 'Do you have a couple of francs you could lend us? I don't like to ask, only we've eaten nothing all day.'

Marius nodded. He had little enough money of his own, but was too kind-hearted to refuse. He put his hand in his pocket, and pulled out a five franc piece.

'Will this be any help?'

As he spoke, Éponine stepped closer to Marius and placed her thin hand on his arm.

'Do you know, Monsieur Marius, you're a very good-looking boy?' He blushed, and she bent forward to whisper in his ear. 'A little bird has told me you're on the look-out for an old man and his pretty daughter,' she said, 'who used to walk in the Luxembourg Gardens a while back. Well, you're in luck. I know her address, if you want it.'

He took Éponine's hands in his. 'How can I ever thank you?' he said. As soon as she gave him the details of the house in the Rue Plumet, Marius set off to search for the girl he thought he had lost forever.

After he had left her, poor Éponine stood for a long time, deep in thought. She had never known anyone like Marius before – polite, generous and kind. She wondered whether he could ever return her feelings for him.

The Rue Plumet is a difficult district to explore if you do not know it well, and Marius struggled to find the house to which Éponine had directed him. As he stood staring at the street signs, a boy about eleven years old, pale faced and lively, trotted up to him.

'Gavroche, sir, at your service!' he said. The boy wore second-hand clothes given to him out of charity – a man's trousers and a woman's blouse. Marius guessed he was one of the many street children to be found in Paris at that time, who lived from day to day, finding food and shelter where they could.

'Can I help you, mister?' the boy asked.

When Marius explained what he was looking for, Gavroche soon took him to the house that Éponine had described.

Marius gave him a few francs – all the money he had left in his pockets.

'Do you live round here, sonny?' he asked.

Gavroche laughed merrily. 'My ma and pa kicked me out years ago! I live where I can, how I can. Anyway, thanks to you I'll eat tonight, and after that, who cares?'

The boy skipped off, a smile filling his pinched face. 'Thanks, mister!' he called over his shoulder.

By a stroke of good fortune, when Marius arrived at the house in the Rue Plumet he decided that he would not go straight to the front door. Instead, he circled the building until he came to the private walled garden which lay at the back of the house – and there to his delight was Cosette. She was sitting reading a book. When she heard a quiet footstep, she looked up to see Marius standing before her.

Cosette, near to fainting, did not utter a sound. As she swayed and closed her eyes, Marius caught her and held her tightly in his arms without realising that he did so. He was overcome with emotion.

'Do you love me?' he stammered.

She answered in a voice almost too low to be heard. 'Of course! You know I do.'

For a long moment they sat together in silence, then gradually began to speak. They told each other about their dreams, how they had felt when they had first met in the Luxembourg Gardens, and their despair when they could no longer see each other.

When everything had been said, she laid her head on his shoulder. 'My name is Cosette. What is yours?'

'Marius.'

For almost two months the two young people met in the garden as often as they could, in secret. Cosette was afraid that if her father (for that was how she spoke of Jean Valjean) discovered that she was seeing Marius, he would send the young man away. As for Marius, he never asked about her father, for the same reason.

There was however a much more serious threat to the young couple's happiness than the possible disapproval of Jean Valjean. By the beginning of June 1832, the political situation in France – and in Paris in particular – was becoming very dangerous. King Louis-Philippe was disliked by many people who thought that France should not be ruled by a royal family. There were food shortages and price rises, and an outbreak of cholera which killed thousands. Some thought the disease had been spread by the authorities. Secret societies were set up by students and others who wanted to overthrow the government, and many of Marius' friends were involved, including Courfeyrac and Bahorel.

On the 5th of June, as Marius was returning one evening from his meeting with Cosette in the Rue Plumet, Courfeyrac rushed to meet him.

'Marius! Thank heavens. You must come with us now – the rebellion has started. We're building a barricade in the Rue de la Chanvrerie.'

Marius did not spend long making his decision. He was loyal to his friends, and felt that he had to support them.

By ten o'clock that evening the barricade had been built, on a corner of the street just in front of an old inn. The students ripped up paving stones from the road, and piled them around furniture from the inn. A cartload full of barrels was overturned, and some large timbers used to prop up a nearby wall were laid across the top. Soon the street was blocked with a solid barrier higher than a man.

More people arrived to join the rebels. One was Gavroche, the street urchin – he knew nothing about the rebels' complaints, but was looking forward to some excitement and perhaps a good meal or two. The next was a thin, frail-looking young man in cord trousers, his long hair tucked away under his cap. Another was a white-haired gentleman in his sixties, who clambered over the barricade with the strength of someone much younger. When he joined the others, the first thing that he saw was Bahorel, holding a gun to the head of a man who had his hands tied behind his back.

'This man's a spy!' the student shouted. 'Who wants to shoot him for me?'

The elderly man stepped forward. 'I know him,' he said. 'He's a policeman called Javert.'

Courfeyrac gave him his pistol. 'Very well. Take him to the garden behind the inn, and do it there. Be quick.'

The man who led Inspector Javert away was of course Jean Valjean. When he reached the garden he untied the policeman's hands.

'Go,' he said. 'Over that wall.' When Javert disappeared, Jean Valjean fired his pistol into the air and returned to the barricade.

By the time he had returned to the street, the King's soldiers had arrived and were attacking the rebels. Tall Municipal Guards were clambering over the barricade, their bayonets glittering in the light of burning torches. More soldiers massed behind them, ready to follow.

It was a critical moment – rather like the instant when flood water reaches the top of an embankment and is beginning to spill over. In another few seconds the stronghold might be overcome.

Bahorel rushed at the first man to cross the barricade and shot him at point blank range, then a second man killed the rebel with a bayonet thrust. A giant of a man was about to attack Gavroche, but before he could reach the youngster, the huge Guardsman fell backwards with a bullet in his forehead. Gavroche spun round to see who had saved him – it was Marius, a pistol in his hand.

Marius stood on the eastern edge of the barricade, and could see that the Municipal Guards and Paris soldiers now covered two thirds of its length. They had not yet jumped down into the enclosure beneath, perhaps because they feared a trap. The rebels below kept up a sharp musket fire, but if the soldiers crossed the barricade that would be the end.

At that moment a Municipal Guardsman rushed up to Marius and pointed his musket at him. When he pulled the trigger, the young workman in cord trousers flung himself between them, and was struck by the musket ball.

Marius could see one of the army officers directing his men to enter the rebels' enclosure. As the man waved his sword, Marius noticed that just in front of the inn there was a barrel of gunpowder, used by the rebels to fill their cartridges. The young man slid down the barricade and raced towards the barrel, lifting it up and snatching a burning torch from Courfeyrac.

'Lay down your weapons!' the officer shouted. 'You must surrender – your position is hopeless!'

Marius waved the torch and caught the man's attention. He held up the powder barrel. 'Clear out or I'll blow the whole place up – and myself with it!' he cried.

The officer hesitated. Then he seemed to sense Marius' desperation, and spoke quietly to his men. Soon there were no more soldiers on the barricade. For the moment, the stronghold had been saved. Marius turned to the young person who had saved him. Her cap had fallen off, and he could see that it was not a workman – it was Éponine, and she was badly wounded. As he knelt down beside her, she spoke softly to him.

'I followed you to the barricade because I love you,' she said. 'Kiss me, Marius.'

He did so, and she died in his arms.

Despite the bravery of Marius and his friends, their position soon became hopeless. They had very little ammunition left, and poor Gavroche was killed collecting cartridges from the bodies of soldiers who were lying on the far side of the barricade.

By two o'clock on the morning of the 6th of June there were only a handful of rebels still alive. A shot rang out in the darkness, and another of the students fell to the ground, badly wounded.

'It's Marius!' Courfeyrac cried. 'Someone take him to the cellar.'

Jean Valjean scooped up Marius as if he weighed no more than a doll, and took him down the cellar stairs. But when the old man was about to return to the barricade, there was an ominous silence above him. The soldiers had made their final attack, and all the remaining rebels were either dead or prisoners.

The reader of this story will no doubt be wondering what happened to the Thénardiers after Jean Valjean had taken Cosette away from them. They had received the justice they deserved for their ill-treatment of the little girl. The Thénardiers became bankrupt, and had left the village of Montfermeil to move to Paris. There they turned to a life of crime, and were sent to prison. Madame Thénardier died shortly afterwards. As for Monsieur Thénardier, he had taken advantage of the confusion and panic caused by the uprising and escaped from his cell.

By three o'clock that morning the police were on Thénardier's trail, and he was on the lookout for a deserted building in which to hide. By chance he came upon the tavern in the Rue de la Chanvrerie – it seemed safe enough, now that the rebels and soldiers had all left. He entered the inn with the police close behind.

Monsieur Thénardier saw Marius stretched out on the floor, his forehead covered in blood, hardly breathing. Jean Valjean's purse was open in front of him – he was checking to make sure he had enough money to take Marius to a place of safety.

'Ho!' cried Thénardier. 'I can see you've killed that young man and grabbed his cash! Well, you're in luck. There's no one around outside. Give me half the loot, and I'll keep quiet. But you'd better hurry.'

Jean Valjean could easily have overpowered the puny little man, but he could not risk making a noise. He gave Thénardier a handful of notes, picked up his wounded companion, and mounted the cellar stairs.

Meanwhile Thénardier had managed to tear a strip of cloth from the corner of Marius' coat. 'Just in case I get the chance to blackmail that murderer again,' he thought.

Jean Valjean reached the back door of the inn and stepped into the overgrown garden. He felt a powerful hand on his shoulder. It was Inspector Javert, alone, with a pistol in his hand.

Six months after the events described above, it might be expected that Jean Valjean would be once again back in prison. After all, when Inspector Javert had found him in the garden of the inn, the old man was still wanted by the police. So why was he not in jail? The answer is simple. He had spared Javert's life – so the Inspector, despite his devotion to duty, had allowed him to go free. Jean Valjean had taken Marius to his grandfather, who decided to forget all about the quarrel that he had had with his grandson. Marius had no idea who had rescued him – he could remember nothing that had happened after he was shot.

Marius gradually recovered from his serious wound. Better still, the French government had decided that they would no longer prosecute or arrest anyone who had taken part in the uprising. Marius and Cosette told Jean Valjean about their love for each other, and he agreed to their marriage. Their wedding day was fixed for 16th February 1833. Jean Valjean announced that Cosette would have a large fortune – over 600,000 francs – and the young couple's future happiness seemed secure.

Although Marius and Cosette were blissfully happy, Jean Valjean was a troubled man. He felt that it was only right for Marius to know the truth about him.

The day before the wedding he asked to speak to Marius, and told him the simple facts – that his real name was Jean Valjean, and that he was a wanted convict, who might be found out and arrested at any time.

Marius was horrified. 'Cosette must never know of this,' he said. 'We must keep your dreadful secret from her. She loves and respects you, and if she learns the truth it will destroy her happiness forever. This is what we must do. After Cosette and I are married, you will have to tell her that she has her own life to live, and that you do not wish to spend too much time with us. She may find it strange at first, but you must arrange things so that Cosette and I will see very little of you. And I cannot accept your 600,000 francs – not from a convicted criminal. I have some money of my own, and it is better that Cosette and I live on that rather than benefit from the proceeds of crime.'

Jean Valjean was heartbroken. Not to see his beloved Cosette! It was almost too much for him to bear. Marius and Cosette looked so happy in each other's company.

Then, after the wedding, some good luck came Valjean's way, and from a most unexpected direction – from Monsieur Thénardier.

By chance Thénardier had seen the wedding procession of the young couple, and had spotted Jean Valjean next to Marius and Cosette. He tracked Marius down, and met with him.

'You don't know my name,' Thénardier said, 'but I've got some news for you, but it'll cost you 5,000 francs to keep me quiet! Your father-in-law, the so-called Monsieur Fauchelevant, is Jean Valjean, a criminal and a murderer! And I've got two pieces of evidence to prove it.'

The first was an ancient and yellowed newspaper cutting from 1823 which described the arrest of a man who had called himself 'Père Madeline', and who had done great things for the town of Montreuil-sur-mer when he was mayor. He had turned out to be an escaped convict, Jean Valjean. The report mentioned that 'as well as giving away large sums to the poor, the mayor had saved over 600,000 francs from the profits of his business'. The second was a strip of cloth torn from the coat of the young man he had seen in the cellar, who Thénardier swore had been murdered by Jean Valjean.

Monsieur Thénardier was astonished at the effect these items had on the young man, who seemed delighted. Marius recognised the cloth – it was from the coat he was wearing when he had been wounded at the barricades. The mysterious stranger who had saved his life was Jean Valjean! As for the 600,000 francs, it was clear that they had been earned honestly. Now he could believe that his father-in-law had turned his back on crime.

As soon as Marius had thrown Thénardier out of the house he ran to Cosette and explained everything that had happened. They ordered their carriage and drove as quickly as possible to the Rue Plumet.

Jean Valjean's housekeeper met them with some sad news. 'My poor master has eaten nothing for days,' she said. 'I wanted to send for the doctor, but he wouldn't let me. And he told me I wasn't to send for you.'

When they knocked on the sitting room door, a feeble voice called 'Come in!' Cosette rushed into the room with Marius close behind.

'Cosette!' said Jean Valjean and sat up in his chair, his face pale and thin. Cosette fell into his arms. 'Father!' she cried.

'So you have both forgiven me?' he said with a trembling voice.

'There is nothing to forgive,' said Marius. 'But why did you not tell me that you saved my life – and that you made your fortune honestly, when you were mayor of Montreuil-sur-mer?'

Jean Valjean shook his head. 'I thought it would be better for both of you if you forgot all about me.'

Cosette laughed. 'Nonsense! You will come home with us now, and get well again, and live with us always.'

Although Jean Valjean was now reconciled
with his beloved Cosette and her husband, the
future that she had wished for was not to be.
A few days later the old man died in peace,
amongst those he loved best. He was buried in
the corner of a quiet churchyard. In accordance
with Jean Valjean's wishes, the stone that
marks his grave has no name upon it.

TAKING THINGS FURTHER

The real read

This *Real Reads* version of *Les Misérables* is a retelling of Victor Hugo's famous original work. If you would like to read the full story, many complete translations of this book are available, from bargain paperbacks to beautiful hardbacks. You should be able to find a copy in your local library, book shop or charity shop. If you can read French, or if you ever decide to study the language, the original French version has the same title.

Filling in the spaces

The loss of so many of Victor Hugo's original words is a sad but necessary part of the shortening process. We have had to make some difficult decisions, omitting subplots and details, some important, some less so, but all interesting. We have also, at times, taken the liberty of combining two events into one, or of giving a character words or actions that originally belong to another. The points below will fill in some of the gaps, but nothing can beat the original.

- We are told about Jean Valjean's time in prison when he was a young man, and about what happened to him before he arrived in Montreuil-sur-mer. He robs a clergyman – Bishop Myriel – but the bishop forgives him and does not hand him over to the police. This experience helps to turn Jean Valjean away from a life of crime.

- We learn more about Fantine, and about the hard life she lives when she is abandoned by Cosette's father. After Fantine sends Cosette to the Thénardiers, they trick Fantine into sending them more and more money.

- When Jean Valjean and Cosette have to leave the Gorbeau tenement because Inspector Javert is on their track, they hide in the grounds of a convent. Jean Valjean gets a job there as a caretaker and he and Cosette live in a cottage nearby. Victor Hugo tells us a great deal about the nuns and about life in the convent.

- Gavroche, who was abandoned by his parents, turns out to be the son of Monsieur and Madame Thénardier. His story shows us the life led by the street children of Paris.

- Marius' father was a colonel at the battle of Waterloo, in 1814. The original version contains a detailed description of the battle, and we are told more about Marius' relationship with his father and his grandfather.

- Éponine, who lives next door to Marius, is the daughter of Monsieur and Madame Thénardier, who moved out of their inn when they became bankrupt. The Thénardiers live by begging, and use 'Jondrette' as their surname. They trick Jean Valjean into going to their rooms, and they try to force him to give them money, but he escapes from them and their gang.

- When Jean Valjean rescues Marius, they escape by using the network of underground sewers below the streets of Paris – these are described in great detail. After Javert decides to let Jean Valjean go free, Inspector Javert drowns himself in the river, because he feels he has failed in his duty as a police officer.

● The original version gives more information about the reasons for the 1832 June Rebellion in Paris, and there is more description of the fighting between the students and the soldiers.

Back in time

The original version of *Les Misérables* starts with an epigraph – a short paragraph telling the reader about the purpose of the book. Victor Hugo uses this to explain to his readers that he wants to write about the 'ignorance and poverty' which he believes has created a 'human hell' for many people.

Les Misérables is often referred to as a historical novel, but when it was published in 1862 the period it describes was well within living memory. Victor Hugo was born in 1802, and would have been a young man in the 1820s and early 1830s when the main events of the story are set. Conditions for poor people in Paris – and in France and the rest of Europe – had not improved much by the 1860s. There was no proper system for helping those who were too old or sick to work, or children who were orphans, or had been abandoned by their parents. Jean Valjean is of course a fictional character, but when he is forced to steal a loaf of bread for his sister's children – or see them starve – he finds himself in the same dreadful situation as many other people during the nineteenth century.

The prison system in France which is described in the book was very different from the kind we have in Western Europe today. Victor Hugo believed that punishing minor offences with long and harsh sentences turned ordinary people into hardened criminals. In this story it is only a lucky chance that saves Jean Valjean from a life of lawlessness and despair.

Victor Hugo was already a famous author when *Les Misérables* was published, and the book quickly became a best-seller, with crowds of people queuing up to buy it. As a result of the descriptions of poverty and misery in the book, the French Parliament passed some new laws about the treatment of criminals, the care of orphans and the education of poor children. Like Charles Dickens' *Oliver Twist*, Victor Hugo's great novel made it much harder for people to ignore the suffering of those less fortunate than themselves.

Finding out more

We recommend the following books and websites to gain a greater understanding of Victor Hugo and the world he lived in.

Books

- Graham Robb, *Victor Hugo*, Picador, 1997. This very thorough and detailed biography is no longer in print, but second hand or library copies can often be found.

- Victor Hugo, *Notre-Dame de Paris (The Hunchback of Notre-Dame)*, Penguin Classics, 2004. One of Victor Hugo's best known books.

Websites

- www.online-literature.com/victor_hugo Details of Victor Hugo's life and work, with links to some of his best known books.

Films

- *Les Misérables* (1978), directed by Glenn Jordan. This is a film version of the original story, not the musical adaptation. It was reissued on DVD in 2013.

- *Les Misérables* (2013), directed by Tom Hooper. This is a film of the musical version of the story. The musical is of course also performed in the theatre.

If you are able to watch one or both of these – or to see the musical on stage – try to spot the differences between these versions and the original story. Why do you think these changes have been made?

Food for thought

Here are a few things to think about if you are reading *Les Misérables* alone, or ideas for discussion if you are reading it with friends.

In retelling *Les Misérables* we have tried to recreate, as accurately as possible, Victor Hugo's original plot and characters. We have also tried to imitate aspects of his style. Remember, however, that this is not the original work; thinking about the points below, therefore, can help you to begin to understand Victor Hugo's craft. To move forward from here, turn to the full-length version of *Les Misérables* and lose yourself in his exciting and imaginative story.

Starting points

- How does Victor Hugo show the reader that Jean Valjean is a good man who has turned his back on a life of crime?

- Do you think that Inspector Javert was right to let Jean Valjean escape, when he was still wanted by the police?

- What does the book tell us about the hard life led by poor people in nineteenth century Paris?

- Some readers have complained that the book contains too many unlikely incidents and coincidences. Did you notice any? Does this matter?

- At the end of the book Jean Valjean says that Marius and Cosette would be better off without him. Why does he think this?

Themes

What ydo ou think Victor Hugo is saying about the following themes in *Les Misérables*?

- poverty and its effects on people

- love

- crime and the criminal justice system

- friendship and loyalty

Style

Can you find paragraphs containing examples of the following?

- descriptions of someone's appearance which give us clues about their character and personality

- realistic or vivid speech which helps us to picture the speaker in our minds

- sections of the story where the author comments directly to the reader

- dramatic scenes which add excitement to the story

Look closely at how these paragraphs are written. What do you notice? Can you write a paragraph in the same style?